CITY OF WHISPERS

L. M. Nightshade

GLOBAL
PUBLISHING
SOLUTIONS

CITY OF WHISPERS by L. M. Nightshade

Published by Global Publishing Solutions, LLC
923 Fieldside Drive
Matteson, Illinois 60443
www.globalpublishingsolutions.com

This book or parts thereof may not be reproduced in any form, stored in a retrieval system, or transmitted in any form by any means—electronic, mechanical, photocopy, recording, or otherwise—without prior permission of the publisher, except as provided by United States of America copyright law.

Copyright © 2024 by L. M. Nightshade

All rights reserved.

International Standard Book Number:
979-8-3302-6952-5
E-book International Standard Book Number:
979-8-3302-7755-1

Unless otherwise indicated, all the names, characters, businesses, places, events, and incidents in this book are either the product of the author's imagination or used in a fictitious manner. Any resemblance to actual persons, living or dead, or actual events is purely coincidental.

TABLE OF CONTENTS

The Enigmatic Arrival 1
Echoes of the Past 4
Veiled Realms 7
The Journey to the Heart 13
Celestial Confluence 17
Ethereal Alchemy 21
The Final Revelation 27
Epilogue: A City Transformed 31

TABLE OF CONTENTS

The Enigmatic Arrival 1
Echoes of the Past 4
Veiled Realms 7
The Journey to the Heart 13
Celestial Confluence 17
Ethereal Alchemy 21
The Final Revelation 27
Epilogue: A City Transformed 31

THE ENIGMATIC ARRIVAL

In the heart of a bustling metropolis, a city materialized overnight, its presence a whispered secret that echoed through the unsuspecting streets. Alex, a resident, awoke to a dawn that carried with it an aura of mystique. The city of whispers had arrived silently, leaving the once-familiar skyline forever changed.

As Alex gazed out the window of their apartment, they saw the enigmatic city stretching across the horizon—an urban labyrinth that seemed to materialize from the shadows. The buildings, adorned with mysterious symbols and ethereal lights, beckoned to the curious with an allure that defied explanation. The structures varied from towering spires that touched the sky to quaint cottages that seemed to belong to another time. Every surface shimmered with an iridescent glow, and intricate patterns seemed to pulse with life, as if the buildings themselves were alive and breathing.

Venturing outside, Alex encountered neighbors and strangers alike, all sharing a bewildered gaze directed toward the city of whispers. Rumors and speculations filled the air as the residents attempted to comprehend the surreal arrival. Some whispered of ancient prophecies, while others believed the city to be a manifestation of collective dreams. The streets were abuzz with conversations, a mix of fear and excitement, as people tried to make sense of the inexplicable phenomenon.

Fueled by an insatiable curiosity, Alex embarked on a journey through the city's labyrinthine streets. Each corner held secrets, and the very air seemed to hum with an otherworldly energy. Alex sensed a cosmic presence, an unseen force that whispered enigmatic tales through the city's every nook and cranny. The alleys twisted and turned unpredictably, leading to hidden courtyards filled with peculiar flora that glowed softly under the morning light.

As the day unfolded, the city of whispers revealed glimpses of its peculiar nature. Statues whispered cryptic messages, and the wind carried echoes of voices long gone. Alex felt a connection, a resonance with the city that transcended the ordinary, setting the stage for a journey into the heart of an enigma that had woven itself into the very fabric of reality. The city had arrived, and its mysteries awaited those willing to listen to its whispers. As the sun set, the city took on a new dimension, with lights illuminating pathways and creating shadows that seemed to move with a life of their own. Alex knew that the true adventure was just beginning.

ECHOES OF THE PAST

As Alex delved deeper into the city of whispers, the streets themselves seemed to whisper tales of ages long past. Buildings bore marks of architectural styles spanning centuries, and murals painted on city walls depicted scenes that echoed with forgotten histories. Each step through the labyrinthine alleys became a journey through time. The cobblestones beneath Alex's feet felt ancient, worn smooth by countless footsteps over the ages. The city seemed to exist out of time, a place where past, present, and future converged.

Exploration led to hidden courtyards adorned with ancient symbols, where the echoes of long-forgotten conversations lingered in the air. Alex encountered residents who spoke of ancestral memories surfacing, as if the city itself held the key to unlocking the past. Some claimed to remember lives they had never lived, recalling events and places from eras long gone. The enigma of the city deepened, and Alex felt a connection to the collective memories embedded within its very stones. It was as if the city was a living repository of human history, preserving the essence of countless souls.

In a tucked-away library, Alex discovered volumes that spoke of a city lost in the annals of time—a place that existed beyond the constraints of linear history. Whispers of mystical societies, legendary figures, and cosmic events permeated the pages. The city of whispers, it seemed, was a living chronicle, weaving the threads of countless tales into its urban tapestry. Each book revealed new layers of mystery, from the exploits of ancient heroes to the rituals of forgotten cults, all connected by the city's enigmatic presence.

Venturing further, Alex encountered apparitions of figures from different eras—ghostly echoes of lives intertwined with the city's fate. These specters shared fragments of their stories, revealing how the city had been a silent witness to triumphs, tragedies, and the ebb and flow of civilization. Some spirits were friendly, eager to share their knowledge, while others were tormented, trapped in their own personal hells. Alex felt a growing responsibility to understand and honor these spectral remnants.

As day turned to night, the city illuminated with a soft glow, and the echoes of the past intensified. The stars above seemed to mirror constellations etched into the city's very foundation. Alex realized that the enigmatic arrival was not merely a city but a living entity, a guardian of memories and a keeper of forgotten lore. This journey through the city's historical echoes revealed a layer of the enigma that bound the present to a myriad of yesterdays. The city's past, intricately interwoven with the present, became a source of both wonder and intrigue, setting the stage for an exploration that transcended the boundaries of conventional time and history. The more Alex learned, the more they felt a part of the city's grand narrative.

VEILED REALMS

In the heart of the city of whispers, Alex uncovered hidden portals that transcended the boundaries of the material world. Veiled realms, accessible only to those attuned to the cosmic energies coursing through the city, beckoned the curious to explore dimensions beyond mortal comprehension. The portals were disguised as ordinary doorways or mirrors, shimmering slightly when viewed out of the corner of the eye. It was only by tuning into the city's subtle vibrations that Alex could perceive their true nature.

Guided by a subtle pull from the city's enigma, Alex discovered a concealed doorway tucked away in an obscure alley. As they stepped through, reality seemed to ripple, and Alex found themselves in a surreal landscape—an otherworldly dimension where the laws of physics and metaphysics intertwined. The sky was a swirl of colors, with floating islands and rivers of light creating a dreamlike panorama. Gravity was fluid, and the air was filled with the scent of unknown flowers.

The veiled realms revealed themselves as ethereal landscapes, bathed in hues unseen by mortal eyes. Alex encountered beings of pure energy, guardians of these hidden dimensions who existed at the intersection of dreams and reality. Conversations with these celestial entities unveiled the city's role as a cosmic nexus—a place where the veiled realms touched the material world. These beings, known as the Luminous Ones, shared knowledge of the cosmic forces that shaped existence and hinted at the delicate balance maintained by the city.

As Alex traversed through these concealed dimensions, they witnessed surreal vistas where time flowed like a cosmic river. Celestial gardens bloomed with flowers that pulsed with the heartbeat of the universe, and fountains of light danced in harmonious rhythms. The veiled realms were a sanctuary, a cosmic tapestry woven with threads of dreams and cosmic energies. Alex felt a profound sense of awe and wonder, recognizing that these realms held answers to questions they had never thought to ask.

Yet, shadows lurked on the edges of these realms—distorted reflections that hinted at an impending imbalance. The guardians whispered of an ancient cosmic force, an enigma that sought to exploit the veiled realms for its nefarious purposes. Alex realized that the cosmic harmony of the city hung in the delicate balance between the wonders of the veiled realms and the encroaching shadows that sought to disrupt it. The guardians spoke of a prophecy, hinting that Alex's arrival was not by chance but by design.

Navigating the surreal landscapes of the veiled realms, Alex encountered celestial beings and gained insights into the city's cosmic significance. The enigma deepened, and the protagonist grappled with the responsibilities that came with being a custodian of the veiled realms—a guardian of the delicate balance between the extraordinary and the encroaching shadows that threatened to disrupt the cosmic harmony. Alex's journey through the veiled realms was both a test and a revelation, preparing them for the challenges that lay ahead.

THE JOURNEY TO THE HEART

The days turned into weeks, and the quantum connection between Emily and David deepened. What began as an enigmatic encounter with an ancient amulet now evolved into a silent symphony of thoughts and emotions that echoed through the corridors of time.

Emily, sitting by the glow of her computer screen, felt an urge to share her world with David in a more tangible form. The quantum connection, while ethereal and enchanting, begged for a more grounded expression. Inspired by an old-world charm, she decided to put pen to paper, writing her thoughts and dreams in letters that transcended the boundaries of time.

In the quiet of her study, surrounded by the scent of ink and the soft rustling of paper, Emily began crafting a letter. The words flowed effortlessly as she narrated the stories of her days—the thrill of unraveling cosmic mysteries, the warmth of a morning coffee, and the quiet contemplation beneath a canvas of stars.

With each stroke of the pen, Emily felt a sense of connection that surpassed the digital whispers of the quantum realm. These letters, tangible and timeless, became vessels carrying the essence of her existence, intended to traverse the quantum expanse and reach David in a realm where the ticking of clocks held no dominion.

As Emily sealed the first letter with an antique wax seal, she couldn't shake the feeling that, in doing so, she was not just sending words but a piece of her soul across the cosmic currents.

On the other side of the quantum connection, David, too, felt the impulse to manifest his thoughts in a tangible form. Inspired by Emily's gesture, he embarked on the art of letter writing—a practice seemingly lost in the digital age. His words, carefully chosen and imbued with the spirit of a fellow explorer, flowed onto parchment.

In his letters, David spoke of the wonders of scientific discovery, the dance of particles, and the ceaseless pursuit of understanding the mysteries that bound the universe together. Each sentence carried the weight of his passion, a passion that reached across dimensions and beckoned Emily to join him in the exploration of the cosmos.

Through the exchange of these timeless letters, Emily and David discovered a connection that transcended the immediate and the ephemeral. The paper, once silent and still, now bore witness to a dance of words that spanned across ages—a dance that celebrated the beauty of human connection in a world where time was but a fleeting illusion.

The letters, suspended in the quantum currents, became a testament to a love story written in ink and sealed with the promise of a connection that would endure the test of time. As Emily and David continued to exchange their handwritten expressions, the cosmic dance of their intertwined destinies gained momentum, propelling them further into the unexplored realms of the heart and the quantum unknown.

CELESTIAL CONFLUENCE

In the heart of the city of whispers, a celestial confluence was foretold—a cosmic event that would align the city's energies with the very fabric of the universe. The enigma's influence intensified as the celestial convergence drew near, and Alex found themselves at the center of a cosmic phenomenon that transcended mortal comprehension. The city itself seemed to pulse with anticipation, its structures vibrating with a resonance that echoed through the streets.

Guided by the city's whispers and celestial alignments, Alex journeyed to a sacred site where the convergence would reach its zenith. This place, known as the Celestial Nexus, was a hidden sanctuary adorned with symbols that mirrored the constellations above. The nexus was a convergence point, a place where cosmic energies interwove with the city's enigma, creating a portal to the stars. The air was charged with anticipation, and the sky above shimmered with an otherworldly glow.

As the celestial event unfolded, Alex witnessed a breathtaking display of cosmic forces. The skies above the city transformed into a canvas of swirling galaxies and radiant stars. Celestial beings, guardians of the cosmic balance, descended upon the city, their presence a testament to the enigma's significance in the grand tapestry of the universe. These beings, known as the Astral Custodians, were embodiments of cosmic harmony, and their arrival signaled the importance of the event.

The convergence revealed the city's true nature—a nexus of cosmic energies that connected the mortal realm to the vast expanse of the universe. Alex stood at the epicenter, feeling the cosmic currents flowing through their very being. The enigma's whispers reached a crescendo, revealing insights into the interconnectedness of all things. Alex understood that the city was not merely a physical space but a living entity, a cosmic crucible where energies from different dimensions converged.

However, the celestial confluence also drew the attention of the clandestine society. Their ambitions threatened to disrupt the delicate balance, and Alex found themselves entangled in a cosmic struggle for control. The Syndicate's leaders, driven by a desire to harness the convergence's power, sought to exploit the city's energies for their own ends. The stakes were higher than ever, and the protagonist's journey became a battle to protect the cosmic harmony that the city represented.

As the celestial event reached its peak, the city's residents gathered to witness the cosmic spectacle. The air was filled with awe and wonder as the celestial beings interacted with the enigma's energies, creating a harmonious symphony of light and sound. Alex, guided by the wisdom gained through their journey, faced the clandestine society in a confrontation that would determine the fate of the city and its cosmic significance.

In the final moments of the celestial confluence, Alex tapped into the enigma's true power, channeling the cosmic energies to restore balance. The clandestine society's ambitions were thwarted, and the celestial beings acknowledged Alex's role as a guardian of the city's harmony. The convergence left an indelible mark on the city of whispers, forever altering its place in the cosmic order.

ETHEREAL ALCHEMY

In the aftermath of the celestial confluence, the city of whispers resonated with ethereal energies that seemed to dance through its every nook and cranny. Alex, now more attuned than ever to the enigma's cosmic currents, embarked on a journey of ethereal alchemy—a quest to understand and harness the transformative powers that had been awakened within the city. The air was charged with a palpable energy, and Alex felt a deep connection to the cosmic forces that permeated the city.

Guided by an intuitive sense of purpose, Alex sought out hidden sanctuaries where the ancient art of ethereal alchemy was practiced. These sanctuaries, concealed in forgotten corners and secret gardens, held the wisdom of generations of alchemists who had devoted their lives to understanding the interplay between cosmic energies and mortal existence. Each sanctuary was a haven of tranquility, where the boundaries between the physical and ethereal blurred, and the air was filled with the scent of rare herbs and the soft hum of cosmic resonance.

In a secluded courtyard bathed in the soft glow of the enigma, Alex encountered an ethereal alchemist—a wise and enigmatic figure who had spent lifetimes unraveling the secrets of the cosmic forces that permeated the city. The alchemist revealed that the city of whispers was a living entity, a cosmic crucible where ethereal alchemy could transform both matter and spirit. Their presence radiated a calm and wisdom that transcended time, and their eyes held the knowledge of countless lifetimes.

Under the alchemist's guidance, Alex delved into the practice of ethereal alchemy, blending cosmic elements to create elixirs that resonated with the enigma's energies. Each concoction held the potential to unlock hidden dimensions, heal ancient wounds, and reveal the interconnectedness of all things. The process was intricate, requiring a deep understanding of cosmic principles and an intuitive grasp of the enigma's rhythms. Alex learned to harness the power of celestial essences, crafting potions that could alter perception, mend broken spirits, and reveal hidden truths.

As Alex honed their skills, they discovered that ethereal alchemy was not merely a manipulation of cosmic forces but a harmonious dance with the very essence of the universe. The enigma responded to their alchemical endeavors, revealing glimpses of the cosmic tapestry that interwove mortal and celestial existence. The more Alex practiced, the more they understood that ethereal alchemy was about balance—about finding harmony between the seen and unseen, the material and the ethereal.

However, the clandestine society, ever watchful, sought to disrupt Alex's ethereal alchemy, fearing that such knowledge would tip the balance of power. Shadows converged upon the sanctuaries, and Alex found themselves entangled in a struggle to protect the ancient wisdom that had been entrusted to them. The Syndicate's agents were relentless, using every means at their disposal to undermine Alex's efforts and seize the secrets of ethereal alchemy for themselves.

Through the practice of ethereal alchemy, Alex gained profound insights into the enigma's nature and the city's cosmic significance. The protagonist realized that the city's enigmatic arrival was not a mere happenstance, but a cosmic event destined to transform the very fabric of reality. The journey of ethereal alchemy became a path of cosmic enlightenment, setting the stage for a confrontation that would determine the fate of the city of whispers and its place in the cosmic order. The deeper Alex delved into the mysteries of ethereal alchemy, the clearer it became that their journey was part of a larger cosmic plan.

As the ethereal alchemy reached its zenith, the enigma's true nature was unveiled—a cosmic symphony that resonated with the heartbeat of the universe. Alex stood on the precipice of understanding, ready to face the ultimate revelation and the cosmic confrontation that would shape the destiny of the city of whispers. The city, now more alive than ever, seemed to pulse with anticipation, as if it too was waiting for the culmination of Alex's journey.

CITY OF WHISPERS

THE FINAL REVELATION

The culmination of Alex's journey brought them to the heart of the city of whispers, where the enigma's energy was most potent. Here, the boundaries between the mortal realm and the celestial dimensions blurred, and Alex could feel the cosmic forces converging. The air was thick with anticipation, as if the city itself was holding its breath for the final revelation. The streets were empty, the usual hustle and bustle replaced by an eerie stillness that signaled the significance of the moment.

In the central plaza, where the celestial confluence had taken place, Alex encountered the Astral Custodians once more. They stood in a circle, their robes glowing with the light of distant stars. At the center of the circle lay an ancient, crystalline artifact—the Heart of the Enigma. This artifact was the source of the city's mysterious power, a cosmic relic that connected all dimensions. The Heart pulsed with a rhythm that resonated with Alex's own heartbeat, creating a profound sense of unity.

The Custodians explained that the Heart of the Enigma had been dormant for millennia, waiting for the right moment and the right person to awaken it. They revealed that Alex's journey through the city had not been a series of coincidences but a series of trials designed to prepare them for this moment. Alex was the chosen one, the guardian destined to unlock the Heart's true potential and restore cosmic balance. The Custodians' eyes held a mixture of hope and solemnity, knowing that the fate of the city—and perhaps the universe—rested on this final act.

As Alex approached the Heart, the clandestine society emerged from the shadows, led by a figure known as the Shadow Alchemist. This antagonist sought to seize the Heart's power for their own ends, believing they could reshape reality to their will. A cosmic confrontation ensued, with the Custodians and Alex facing off against the shadowy figures. The plaza became a battleground, with cosmic energies clashing and creating ripples that distorted space and time.

In the midst of the battle, the Heart of the Enigma began to pulse with an intense light. Alex, drawing upon the knowledge and skills gained through their journey, channeled the enigma's energy to combat the Shadow Alchemist. The struggle was fierce, with both sides wielding immense power. The city of whispers seemed to hold its breath, its very existence hanging in the balance as the cosmic forces collided.

As the battle reached its climax, Alex realized that the key to unlocking the Heart's true power lay not in domination but in harmony. They reached out to the Shadow Alchemist, offering a chance at redemption and understanding. The enigma's whispers filled the air, guiding Alex's actions and revealing the interconnectedness of all beings. In a moment of clarity, the Shadow Alchemist hesitated, and the cosmic energies began to harmonize.

With a final surge of energy, Alex and the Shadow Alchemist combined their powers, unlocking the Heart of the Enigma. A blinding light enveloped the plaza, and the city of whispers resonated with a cosmic symphony that echoed across dimensions. The shadows dissipated, and the city was bathed in a radiant glow that signaled the restoration of balance. The Custodians bowed in reverence, acknowledging Alex's role as the guardian of the city's harmony.

The final revelation unveiled the enigma's ultimate truth—a cosmic dance of creation and destruction, balance, and chaos, where every being played a part in the grand tapestry of existence. Alex, now fully attuned to the enigma's essence, understood that the city's enigmatic arrival was a catalyst for cosmic evolution. The journey had come full circle, revealing the profound interconnectedness of all things and the enduring power of harmony.

EPILOGUE: A CITY TRANSFORMED

In the aftermath of the final revelation, the city of whispers stood transformed. The enigmatic arrival had woven itself into the very fabric of reality, leaving an indelible mark on the lives of its inhabitants. The city, once a mystery, had become a beacon of cosmic harmony—a testament to the transformative power of the enigma. The buildings glowed with a soft luminescence, and the air was filled with a sense of peace and unity.

Alex, now the Cosmic Guardian, embraced their role with a sense of fulfillment. They walked through the city's streets, feeling the enigma's presence in every corner. The residents, once bewildered by the city's arrival, now embraced the cosmic energies that permeated their lives. The city had become a sanctuary of knowledge and wisdom, a place where the boundaries between the mortal and celestial realms blurred.

The celestial beings, having fulfilled their purpose, bid farewell to the city, leaving behind a legacy of cosmic enlightenment. The veiled realms remained accessible to those attuned to the enigma's energies, offering glimpses into the mysteries of existence. The clandestine society, now reformed, worked alongside the city's inhabitants to protect the balance and safeguard the ancient wisdom that had been entrusted to them.

In this transformed city, Alex continued their journey, not as a lone explorer but as a guide and protector. They shared the knowledge gained through their trials, teaching others the art of ethereal alchemy and the wisdom of cosmic harmony. The city of whispers had become a living testament to the enduring power of balance, a place where the enigma's whispers continued to guide and inspire.

The journey of the city of whispers was far from over. New mysteries awaited discovery, and new challenges would arise. But with the Heart of the Enigma as its core, the city stood as a beacon of hope and enlightenment, a testament to the transformative power of cosmic harmony. Alex, the Cosmic Guardian, embraced their role with a sense of purpose, knowing that the city's journey was part of a grand cosmic design—a dance of creation and balance that would continue to unfold across the ages.

And so, the city of whispers stood as a symbol of cosmic unity, a place where the enigmatic arrival had woven a tapestry of harmony that resonated across the universe. The journey of Alex and the city was a testament to the power of understanding, balance, and the enduring connection between all things. The enigma's whispers would continue to guide those who listened, revealing the profound truths that lay at the heart of existence.

www.ingramcontent.com/pod-product-compliance
Lightning Source LLC
LaVergne TN
LVHW051923060526
838201LV00060B/4144